HATE IS OF LOVE: THE BUCKINGHAM

CW00407433

BY MALLORIE MELDRUM
Cover by K. Day

HATE IS THE OTHER SIDE OF LOVE:
THE DUKE OF BUCKINGHAM & RICHARD III

BY MALLORIE MELDRUM

The room sweltered, the torches burning low in the brackets on the wall. Even the night air drifting through the windows was humid, a blast from the furnaces of Hell. The sky glinted jet, no stars showing; it was as if a pall hung over the night-time London sky, holding in the unnatural summer heat, smothering the very wind...

Harry Stafford, Duke of Buckingham, glanced over at Richard of Gloucester...no, he was King Richard now, crowned and anointed, by Grace of God King of England, Lord of Ireland. In the privacy of Richard's chambers both men were informal in manner and dress...and struggling with the fierce, cloying heat. Sitting at a table facing Buckingham,

Richard had discarded his gown and doublet, was down to his linen shirt which hung open to his waist. Buckingham had also discarded his top layers or clothing but was not in quite as much disarray as the new King. Richard poured out a glass of wine for himself and then another for his cousin; he pushed the goblet towards Buckingham with a sharp gesture. It was just another one of many cups they had consumed that night; their conversation had been long, drawn out and sometimes heated. And private...the usual servants had been banished hours ago.

Richard's face bore a deeply troubled expression. "How can I deal with the situation I find myself in?" He pushed his hair away from his forehead in an irritated gesture. "What must I do, Harry?"

"You know what must be; I have said it before." Buckingham's eyes glittered, slightly glazed from the consumption of so much alcohol. "Think of it, Richard...what will happen if it is not done. Think of your Edward...and Anne... The House of York."

Richard stared out the window into the darkness; a bead of sweat trickled down his cheek. "I know, Harry....but ...to do this thing...I will be damned...."

"You will be damned if you do not, cousin!"

Richard leaned forward, putting put both elbows on the table and pressing his face against his laced fingers, which were long and pale, rimed by heavy rings. He said nothing, just sat in silence, shoulders stiff. Buckingham watched him, not daring to speak further. Fuelled by the alcoholic fire in his belly, a different sensation of heat suddenly rushed over the twenty-eight year old Duke. His groin tightened and he shifted uncomfortably, glad for the concealment his elaborate codpiece gave him. There was something about him that Richard did not know, that few knew even in his intimate circles. The contempt he felt for his Woodville wife, Catherine, was common knowledge at court but most men believed it was because of her lowly status. Her lesser blood was part of the problem, certainly, but there was more to it than having humble origins. Harry Stafford preferred to lie with men. He had children with the Woodville broodmare, certes, and he loved them and treated them as a father should, but when he could he would inveigle a young squire or a tipsy or curious friend into his bed ....and then they would part in the morning as if nothing had passed between them (Harry was no fool, after all; it was not something one would wish the public to know.)

His eyes narrowed and he let his hand slip across the table to rest on Richard's forearm. He hoped his touch seemed comforting. He had been watching his cousin for a while. He couldn't make him out. He wondered if there was any chance he could get closer to him, closer than he had a right to be....Richard had bastards so he obviously liked to fuck women, but then again...His wife Anne had only borne the one child almost ten years ago, and Richard's byblows had been begotten before his marriage...Who knew who shared his bed these days? Irrational as it was, Buckingham had always felt a smidgen of jealousy towards Dickon's long-time friend Francis Lovell, and was glad when he seemed to be working his way between the two, supplanting Lovell in Richard's favours......

Suddenly Richard let his hands drop from his face. He looked bone weary, shadows underscoring his dark grey-blue eyes. Buckingham scanned his features hungrily. There was something about this small, thin, dark-haired cousin of his, the runt of the litter amongst the golden giants in his family, which moved him unduly. Moved him more than anyone ever had before, and not just in his loins. He wasn't sure just why, though he found it strangely attractive that Richard, with his fine hands and almost pretty features, was at the same time a seasoned soldier...and one who could probably best Buckingham in any martial contest between them.

He took another gulp of wine, his vision blurring and his head starting to spin. He had to get Richard's attention, to make him understand. "Listen," he said, "I will help you in this matter…it will not be on your head then. Do I have your agreement?"

Richard pulled away and abruptly rose from the table, his glass falling over and streaming wine like blood. "No…*no*. I cannot talk more of this dreadful thing, Harry…"

Buckingham followed his cousin across the chamber. Now…it had to be now…. He had to speak while he could, while the courage blazed in him. "Richard, I beg you, listen to me…"

By the far wall, its elaborate tapestries depicting unicorns and maids, Harry Stafford caught the King gently but firmly by the shoulders, turning him towards him.

Richard stared at him quizzically but did not try to pull away. Buckingham grasped Richard's right hand, replete with its many rings, and lifted it to his mouth. He kissed it first as he would his liege lord, but then slowly, turned it over and pressed his lips against the palm. He felt a thrill of sensual pleasure as his mouth brushed the incongruously sword-callused skin on that small, graceful hand and tasted salt. That hand could give him everything…or take it all away.

"Your Grace…" he started formally, but then, fuelled by drink to boldness and over familiarity, "Dickon, my kinsman, know that I love you and would do whatever is needed that all be well and safe for you."

"I am glad of your loyalty, Harry…"

Buckingham leaned in further; one hand slipping from Richard's shoulder onto his bare chest beneath his open shirt. Buckingham shuddered slightly; he could feel his cousin's heartbeat quicken…Could he possibly feel in any wise what he desired? Between his legs Harry's cock was harder than it had even been before. By Christ, he just wanted to turn Richard around, shove him up against the wall, and fuck him until he begged for either mercy or for more!

"Together we can accomplish so much…" Buckingham's fingers trailed down the line of dark hair in the centre of Richard's chest, coming to rest on his lower belly. He had not one ounce of flab on him, unlike his dead brother Edward who had died fat and glutted in his bed surrounding by whining Woodvilles. "You will want for nothing with me by your side. None shall stand against you and win."

Richard said nothing. He did not move, seemed scarcely to breathe, his eyes shaded and unreadable beneath his dark lashes. Buckingham drew a deep noisy breath. "Cousin, let us seal this alliance between us for all time. I beg you, my lord…my beloved lord." He took his hand from Richard's belly and brought it up to tangle it in his long wavy hair. Bending his head he lightly skimmed his lips against Richard's, a chaste enough kiss that would not be grossly unacceptable amongst close family members. But then, this initial testing contact over, he tilted his head to the side and pressed backwards, forcing Richard's mouth open with gentle but firm pressure of teeth and tongue. He could taste the wine they had both been drinking, the spices…Oh God…it was almost too much to bear! He clutched Richard to him, pressing himself against his body, trying clumsily to remove his hose and his cousin's at the same time.

The next moment a blazing pain shot through the side of his face and he found himself sprawled on the ground, his head reeling. Richard stood over him, eyes blazing with a cold deadly fire. He had only seen an expression like that on his cousin's face once before—the day Richard had ordered William Hastings' execution, after Hastings' plotting had been revealed and he had spoken terrible, threatening words. "You forget who I am and you forget your place," he snapped. "Get out and sober up, Harry —you have obviously had too far much to drink!"

Buckingham clawed at his ankles. "Forgive me…" he said, and then, consumed by shame and the surfeit of wine, he began to weep. It shocked him—he was not inclined to tears, at least not real ones. "A madness possessed me. Do not hold it against me….I love you, Richard."

"So you have said," Richard retorted sarcastically. "Now get out before I have you thrown out."

Buckingham scrambled to his feet and staggered out into the corridor. Outside he slumped in a dark niche in the corridor wall, eyes burning, his breath railing raggedly in his lungs. Why…why had this happened? Amidst his embarrassment and shame, a little frisson of anger burned in his heart. Even if Richard had not desired him, why should he strike him like a cur? He would have stepped away the moment Richard had asked him to. How dare he treat him so, when Buckingham had helped him in so many ways and had even offered to rid him of the problem that, unless soon solved, would trouble his reign for years to come?

Anger growing, he stalked down the corridor. "Oh, I shall keep my word, cousin," he muttered to himself. "I will continue to serve you and do what is best for us both. But if you do not learn to treat the one who has served you well with more graciousness, you may find that you come to rue the day I helped to put that pretty crown of gold upon your head!"

***

Richard stormed towards Anne's chambers, uncaring that there were servants abroad who saw him in his agitated and half-dressed state and would doubtless start spreading idle rumours within the hour. Reaching the Queen's apartments, he threw the great wooden door open then slammed it shut behind him, shooting the bolt with a resounding bang. The room was unlit, with only the pale hangings on the bed standing out in the blackness. He heard Anne stir, awoken by his noisy entry. She probably hadn't been expecting him tonight, thinking that his business with the Duke of Buckingham might last well into the small hours of the morning.

"Yes, and what business that turned out to be!" he thought. A burst of fury followed by a flush of embarrassment coursed through him.

He was not used to disrobing himself, and he tore clumsily at his hose and shirt, tearing them off wadded up together and dumping them in a pile on the floor. Flinging the embroidered curtains on the bed aside, he threw himself in beside Anne, who rolled over on her side to face him, her long, unbound hair like a molten river across the sheet. "Richard?" she said sleepily. "Is something amiss?"

"Yes, something is…" He pulled her towards him more roughly than his usual manner. Her slender frame was encased in a voluminous white linen night-gown; beneath the thin cloth her flesh felt overly warm, over-heated, almost feverish. He recalled this heat from Buckingham's nearness, the feverish lust in his eyes, and he suddenly released her and sat up, legs dangling over one side of the bed.

"Richard, you are shaking! What is the matter?" Her arms reached up to circle his waist, drawing him back into the centre of the huge bed with its scents of lavender and herbs.

"It is Harry, Anne. Harry Stafford."

"What has he done?" Anne's voice went a little bit flat. She did not like or trust the Duke of Buckingham, and she knew that Richard's brother Edward had not liked him either—the only Duke to have been given no real position. But Richard obviously loved him, and he had helped so much in his accession to the throne that she dared say nothing against him to her husband.

Richard was silent for a moment. She felt him tense against her. "He…he laid hands on me, Anne."

A little gasp escaped from between her teeth. "You fought with him? He assaulted you…the King?"

"Not…exactly." Richard sounded strained. "Anne…" He shifted himself on top of her; she could just see the outline of his face in the dimness, felt strands of his long hair fall forward to tickle her nose.

"Yes, what is it, husband?" She moved under him, making herself more comfortable and accommodating. His right hand was circling her breast now, not altogether gently, while the other hand dragged her white linen robe up under her armpits. Anne reached up to kiss his mouth...and wondered that he momentarily flinched away, then violently returned the kiss, bruising her lips with his own. What on earth could be wrong?

"Anne..." he said her name again, and she could hear doubt and irritation and confusion mingled in his voice. His fingers dipped between her thighs and she spread them further, opening to him as he caressed her secret place. Warmth flooded her and she bent her knees while he knelt between them. She wanted to touch him as he touched her, but she could already feel his hard cock hot against her leg and she intuited that tonight he was not in the mood for gentle or lengthy caresses in his lovemaking. He wanted to take her, swiftly and efficiently, with little preamble. Sliding his hands under her buttocks, supporting her and lifting her up slightly toward him, he thrust into her with a ferocity that startled her.

She bit back a small squeal of surprise, feeling a slight discomfort at first, for she was not quite ready to take him...but the soreness swiftly vanished as her body adjusted to his movements. A rush of excitement ran through her; he had been so busy since becoming king that he had not had the time for her as he had of old, at Middleham. They had always shared a bed-chamber then, ever since they were married, despite the whispers that it was a 'thing peasants did.' Even now, they spent more nights together than most people of their status, even if only to sleep; but with all of Richard's affairs of state, lately he had not come to her chambers but gone to his own apartments, where he could return late and rise, still red-eyed, before dawn to start another busy day.

Anne wrapped her legs around Richard, pulling him harder against her, enjoying this sweet swordplay of love. She smiled to herself in the darkness; if this was indeed a form of fleshly swordplay, her husband was a skilled swordsman indeed and had driven his blade to the hilt with consummate skill. Jesu, grant her this closeness with her husband again…and maybe, maybe their reign would be blessed by another child, another little prince of the House of York, a brother for young Ned who waited patiently in the North for his Royal parents.

She gave a soft contented sigh, waves of pleasure running through her body from her loins outwards, and at that moment Richard spilled his seed inside her womb with a shudder. She felt warmth trickle down her inner thighs and said a quick prayer; it was rumoured that if a man and wife found pleasure at the same time, it was more likely a child would be conceived.

Too long had she been barren; it would be such a positive sign to the people of England if she could produce another child…

Richard collapsed forward onto her breast, his dark hair sticking in curling tendrils to her soft white flesh, and she held him against her, like the child she so desired. A few moments later he withdrew from her, propped himself up on his elbows and gazed down into her face. She could tell he was still troubled about something. "Anne, you must tell me the truth," he said in a tight voice. "Is there anything about me, anything at all… that would make you think I am a *fucking catamite*?"

His question and his profanity were so unexpected and so outrageous that a burst of nervous laughter tore from her throat. She felt him flinch angrily at the sound, and forced her unbidden mirth to silence. "Why ever are you asking such a question, my love? What a strange thing to ask."

"Why do you think I ask you, Anne?"

She fell silent, deep in thought, and then the answer came. Buckingham…it had to be Buckingham. She had not realised but certainly thought of him as something of a popinjay, though many nobles loved to flaunt their fine clothes and jewels—Richard himself was certainly not averse to dressing in fine velvet and many gems. But there had been a difference in Buckingham's mannerisms and she had noted the way his eyes followed

Richard: hot, almost greedy and devouring. In reverse, he had only ever been coolly polite to Anne, almost making a cipher of her presence, as if she was completely irrelevant.

"So that is what you meant when you said he laid hands on you! What will you do? Send him away?" She tried to keep hopefulness out of her voice.

Richard shook his head. "I cannot, Anne. He is too powerful, and I need him and the men he can bring to my cause. And look how he has helped me…."

"But think about the reasons why he might have done so," she said softly. "If he suspects he has no chance, that he has been thwarted, what might that drive him to do?"

"He will get over this madness, surely." Richard slid from the bed, naked, and walked over to the table to pour himself a flagon of wine. Anne watched him, a white figure in the gloom; his legs were long in comparison to his torso, and she could see, as her eyes adjusted to the dimness, the tilt of his ribcage, the sideways curve of his back. He had borne this flaw since his youth but she was sure it had worsened of late; it hurt him too, he had told her so once, but never had he complained to anyone. "He is Constable of England, and Great Chamberlain…What more does the man want?"

"I think you already know what," said Anne quietly. "The one thing you cannot give him. How he responds will all depend on which is more important to him. His…love…for you or his position in your court."

Richard sighed, draining the wine to the dregs. "And I cannot read his mind or his heart, that is obvious. What a blind fool I have been."

Anne sat up, holding the coverlet around her. "Oh Richard, I beg you, please send him away. I…I just feel there will be no happy ending to this matter."

Richard put down the flagon and walked back to the bed. "We go on progress soon. Plenty of time for Harry to cool his ardour. Do not worry yourself, Anne; I wish I had said nothing to you for I see I have upset you."

She held out her arms to him, and he sank back into the huge bed, curling himself in against her. He slept, but Anne remained awake for a long while, breathing in the scent of his tangled hair, his warm skin, just savouring that moment, before it was gone forever, when he was just Richard, her husband, and not the King of England.

***

"Where is Buckingham?" King Richard's voice was sharp. Arrayed in his finest, with the greatest nobles in the land gathered around him and the Queen ensconced in her litter with her ladies, he was ready to set off on his progress around England, hopefully to win the hearts of the people and banish the doubts that many had over the manner in which he came to the throne. First would be Windsor, then Oxford and its surrounds, where he would visit the house of his friend Francis Lovell, then onwards across the country and up to York, where he had no need to try to win friends for he was already much loved in that mighty northern city. But where was Harry Stafford? As Constable and the second most powerful man in the land, he should have been in attendance and following his king. Richard had shown his displeasure to Buckingham by ignoring him and shunning his presence since the night Harry tried his unwelcome advances, but he had not reprimanded him further or threatened greater consequences, and he would have expected his cousin to be riding beside him.

Suddenly a messenger ran up, breathless; he wore Harry's colours, black and red. A letter was clutched in his hand. "Your Grace." He sank to one knee and proffered the letter.

Richard took the missive, face like thunder. Reading the note, he crumpled it in his gloved hand and cast it contemptuously on the ground. "So he is ill, is he? Too ill to ride out. Well, take my lord of Buckingham a message from me…When he is well I will expect him to make haste and join me on my progress, as is his duty."

The man rose, bowed hastily and ran off, looking fearful as if demons were on his tail. Richard glared sourly at his retreating back, a vague unease rising inside him. He was half minded to go find Harry and drag him from his supposed sick-bed, but he had no time and no real stomach for such unseemly antics.

He had a long journey to make and a kingdom to greet. Turning his face away, he looked to the final preparations before he left the sweltering confines of summer-bound London.

***

Harry Stafford walked through the dusk toward the Tower. Tendrils of fog coiled from the Thames, rising like ghostly hands in the twilight; the river stunk with the wastes hurled into its waters, a vile miasma that reeked faintly of death and decay. He was wearing his finest clothes, and in quite inappropriate colours; his blue doublet was just a bit too close to royal purple, shot through with yellow strands that were almost the hue of gold, the colour worn only by Kings. Richard wasn't around to see his grand display, though, and who would dare to tell him? Harry was the second most important man in the country after the King….and no one suspected that Richard hadn't spoken to him for days.

That saddened Harry. After his first burst of anger at his cousin, he had quieted his violent thoughts. He even blamed himself…a little. Aye, Richard has been harsh with him, but he, Harry, had been thoughtless as well, too forthright, the drink making him foolish and loose-tongued. He should have taken his time, tested Richard slowly, and not pawed at him like some lust-crazed oaf. He was not giving up yet; he would win Richard's gratitude, and then maybe he could win an even greater prize from him…. He paused, taking a deep breath, remembering the feel of Richard's skin beneath his hand, the brief but lingering taste of his mouth. *He did not push me away when I first kissed him*, he thought desperately, convincing himself that it was the truth. *He did not….*

Reaching the adamant foot of the Tower, he forced thoughts of Richard from his head. Desires of the flesh were one thing, but he had another kind of need to attend to tonight. Passing beneath the gloomy arch, already centuries old, he was challenged by Robert Brackenbury, who held the position of Constable of the Tower. He had risen high in Richard's favour too; a quiet and loyal man who had great learning. He glanced at Buckingham, eyes widening slightly with surprise, then bowed briefly. From beneath the brim of his hat

Buckingham stared at the older man with thinly disguised contempt; Brackenbury had a high position but had not even been knighted, so he did not think he would dare question too much…Any other perhaps, but it was not for him to unduly question one as high as the Duke of Buckingham, the king's own kinsman.

"I am here on the King's business," he explained silkily, doffing his hat and giving Brackenbury his most appealing smile. "That is why I am not on progress with His Grace."

"Forgive me…but I had no word of your coming." Brackenbury looked uneasy.

"No, you wouldn't have," said Buckingham curtly, his false smile fading. "And you will tell none that you have seen me here tonight, do you understand? You *will* not, if you love our Lord King."

"I do understand, my Lord." A worried crease lowered Brackenbury's forehead and he stepped back from Buckingham. Cold wind from the open door made the torches dip for a moment, plunging the stairwell and passage beyond into unwelcome dimness. The Duke shivered for a moment, suddenly struck by the age of the place, the weight of years that leaned on those stalwart grey walls…It was as if ghosts of the past were crowding down those ancient worn stairs, watching him, wondering what addition he was making to this stone fortress's long and turbulent history…

Mawkish imaginings! He threw off such dark thoughts, and passing Brackenbury without another glance began to climb the stairs, determination supplanting any fears, any doubts. This *had* to be done…he knew it, and Richard knew it too, wavering though he had been these many days. What Harry planned would be a gift to the King, excusing him and freeing him at the same time. Even if he was upset with Buckingham at first; surely he would soon see the truth.

He reached a large wooden door with two stony-faced guards posted on either side. They did not even dare look at him; he was so far above them. "I am here on the King's business, a matter of great import!" he said tersely. "Let me pass."

They let him pass.

Harry entered a warm, cosy chamber. It was emptier than he remembered, with some furnishings gone; Richard was preparing to move the room's precious contents, perhaps to Sheriff Hutton in the north, perhaps to some unknown secret destination. A child's wooden toy lay on the flagstones; it crunched under Buckingham's boot heel as he walked forward, and he cursed and kicked it aside.

A bed with rich draperies stood against the far wall; he approached it purposefully and yanked the hangings aside. Two young boys lay abed, both golden-haired, one tall, a youth rather than a boy, the other, younger, curled up against his side like a puppy—the bastard sons of dead Edward. *The thorn in everyone's side,* thought Buckingham uncharitably. *Rallying point for rebellion...*

As he watched the elder boy's eyes flickered open. He glanced up at the Duke warily, the lad who had, so briefly, been Edward V, unannointed king of England. Harry's lip curled; the boy was a true Woodville in appearance except that he had inherited his father's height. Same haughty look and hooded eyes as his mother, Elizabeth, and Buckingham's own wife, the annoying and acquisitive Catherine. Same mannerisms as his foppish and now-very-dead uncle, Anthony Woodville, Lord Rivers, who had been a huge influence on Edward while he was ensconced at Ludlow Castle.

"My uncle Buckingham, why are you here at this late hour?" Young Ned sat up, while at his side small Richard also stirred. The elder prince's deep blue eyes were fixed on Buckingham's face; he could see the fear and dislike, even hatred, in their depth. He knew it was rumoured that the brat was in daily terror for his life, though only God knew why...None had laid hands on him or his brother since they were brought to the Tower, and they had even been allowed outside on the lawns to play about shooting at butts.

"It is a secret, young lord," said Buckingham, a cruel smile quirking the corner of his lips. "Dress quickly, in dark clothes…your brother the lord Richard as well…and then follow me, without a sound."

"Are we going to be set free?" asked young Ned, rising. Buckingham could see that he was trembling faintly.

Buckingham smiled again. "Yes, dear nephew, soon you will both be free….there will be naught more to fear in all the world for you. I can promise you that."

***

Buckingham sat in the drafty solar of his castle at Brecknock. He had a pounding headache and felt sick to his stomach. In the next chamber he could hear his children playing noisily, screaming and thumping around in a most unseemly manner. Something crashed, shattered; there was a moment's silence then shrill almost hysterical peals of mirth. The sound of children's laughter made his guts convulse even more; he wanted to be sick into the great fireplace, save that it would make the place reek to high heaven.

In the doorway he saw the shadow of a great steepled henin and then the pallid, disapproving face of his wife Catherine Woodville. She gave him a hard glare then vanished, her stride deliberately purposeful; obviously she thought he should be the one to sort out the ruckus in the next room. She had no idea what was wrong with him, and didn't much care. He wanted to throw something at her haughty retreating posterior but nothing was at hand that he cared to break.

Getting up from his chair, he stormed past Catherine, blocking out her muffled cry of shrewish protest, and descended into the bowels of the castle. He should have joined the King's progress, but in the aftermath of his visit to the Tower he had been genuinely sick, a malady more of the spirit than the body, and had retreated to his holdings to recover...and to think. He had to get a hold of himself; he felt half-mad these days, tormented by lust, by ambition, by all the deeds of this summer in which he had played a part.

For some reason, his feet carried him to the chambers where his prisoner, Bishop John Morton, was held. He peered through the keyhole; the Bishop was sitting inside, quite contentedly, eating a great chicken leg on a trencher and looking rather pleased with himself, as if he really was not too bothered about his state of incarceration. Morton wiped his greasy fingers on his robes and began to hum to himself as he thumbed through a richly illuminated book.

Buckingham had talked to the prisoner on several occasions. At first Morton had played the part of a solicitous churchman, suffering for his faith and ready to give heartfelt advice to his captor. Then came gently prying questions, words with double meanings…lies breathed through silver. Lies…or were they? There was truth in his speech as well, as Morton had said, "Why do you support this usurper, my son? Why do you lend him your strength? Outside of rude North-men, he is not loved. Why, you would be a better choice for King than him…and your claim is good! You, a noble scion of the House of Lancaster…."

Buckingham debated whether to talk to Morton again tonight….but decided against it. Something in the old man's eyes, which were pale grey flecked with yellow, unnerved him. They were almost like serpent's eyes and didn't match the humble, depreciating smile Morton always wore on his creased old face. The eyes and the calm voice and its words of gentle treason were mesmerising. Too mesmerizing. Too tempting

He had to ride out. He had to see Richard. After what he had done for his friend, he surely would reward him. Reward him with his love. That was Buckingham asked.

***

The Duke rode with his retinue toward the town of Gloucester, where the King had stopped while upon his progress. As he neared the town walls, he could see the tall tower of the great cathedral poking the dull blue of the sky, its stonework blazing gold in the summer sun. He felt apprehensive but strangely elated too. In his head he fantasised about the king greeting him with open arms, realizing that he had nearly driven away his wisest and most loyal companion, the one who had helped put him on the throne, who counselled him swift movement where he would have hesitated, who had risked all for him in so many ways. He, in turn, would kneel at Richard's feet in humble homage and kiss his hand...Oh Jesu, yes, kiss his hand, and then he would stay on his knees before Richard indeed, and put his lips to better sport if he were permitted. He grinned to himself, suddenly flushed with lust, his crotch horribly uncomfortable against the saddle. He would wager a fortune that prim, bloodless Anne Neville had never given her husband that kind of pleasure....

Riding into the town, Harry Stafford soon found the inn where the King was staying for the night. The streets were heaving with people trying to catch a glimpse of the new King and Queen; a sea of unwashed humanity that surged like the roll on the river. Piemen hawked their wares from hastily set up stalls, while old crones sold sprigs of flowers to hold up against the stench of the nearby Severn, running low and foetid in the summer heat. Urchins ran amok in the crowds, picking pockets at will until the town guards were alerted and chased them screaming into dark alleyways between the tall, timber-framed houses. A few townsfolk glanced up curiously as the Duke of Buckingham and his men pushed through the throng, wondering about the identity of this haughty, proud-looking man, dressed in clothes nigh as fine as those worn by the new King, who had addressed the crowds in the town square earlier that day, announcing that he would make Gloucester a county in its own right, with a mayor and Alderman, and presenting the town with a gift of a great sword of much beauty and worth.

Buckingham ignored the stares; he was used to them. Although inclined to put on weight and to be florid-faced when he drank or ate too much, he was a handsome man, well built with dusky gold curls falling below his collar, all set off by his magnificent cloak and doublet and hat, and his flashing collar of gems. He was used to being admired…but lately it was all like cold ashes in his mouth. He had admiration and envious looks but Harry Stafford did not have what he really craved…

Reaching the inn where Richard was spending the night, he dismounted his steed, casting his reins to the ostlers and ordering them curtly to give his horse the best of care. Bright as a peacock, with his crimson cloak flaring out behind him, he ploughed through the hordes of people milling about the cobbled courtyard; the King's men, the innkeeper's family, dozens of servants both from the inn itself and from the royal household. Several huge barrels were of wine were being noisily rolled across the flagstones into the door of the inn, doubtless for King Richard and his most loyal followers.

Harry grinned. He approved—good wine could lose a man's tongue and his inhibitions.

Entering the inn, he beckoned to the fat, balding innkeeper, red and sweating like some pig in the excitement of the day. "Where is his Grace the King?" he said haughtily.

"Who wants to know?" the man bleated, waving his arm at his kitchen boys as they hauled in supplies and stoked the ovens.

Buckingham raised his eyebrows and gave the bloated old fool an evil look, and touched the chain of office gleaming around his neck. "I am the Duke of Buckingham," he said icily, each word clipped and spoken slowly as if he were talking to an idiot.

The man's face purpled and he made a small, apologetic bow and gestured to a side corridor. "Forgive me, your Grace. The King is in there, my Lord."

The Duke turned on his heel and strode down the corridor, pushing pot-boys and tavern wenches aside in his wake. He reached a second inner courtyard, this one private, away from the tumult of the inn, and better kept. The flagstones were swept clean and washed down, and flowers climbed the faces of the buildings, casting off a sweet, sultry fragrance that warred with the unwholesome scent of the nearby river and the teeming town.

The King was standing before an arched door. Sunlight streamed over the rooftops above, playing over the contours of his face and catching the ruddy hues in his thick dark hair. Buckingham paused for a minute, staring. Richard was wearing a red velvet gown trimmed with gold; his long sleeves were shot with deep green silk. A collar of golden links circled his shoulders; little white roses were mounted on it, their hearts flashing sapphires. Around the roses, sprays of garnets clustered like blood-drops, shimmering in the warm late afternoon sunlight. He looked slightly weary but well and happy. His usual crowd of followers were close around him, Buckingham noted sourly—Francis Lovell on his right, laughing as he raised a glass to his lips; sharp-eyed Ratcliffe who missed nothing; and the lawyer Catesby with his expressionless, give-naught-away eyes, who had worked for Buckingham once…and also for dead Hastings some of whose lands found their way into Catesby's hands. Buckingham's lip curled. He knew they would all be there, but they were faces he'd rather not see; he knew they distrusted him, even his former servant Catesby, who even now turned and peered at him with his blank, unreadable expression and nodded with false courtesy. *Typical lawyer*, Harry thought with disdain.

Richard glanced up. Buckingham scanned his face, anxious to read his thoughts. He saw a flicker of annoyance, as might be expected since he had come so late to the progress, and for a moment fear gripped his guts, but then a small smile turned up the corners of Richard's thin lips. "Well…look who is has come to join us at last," he said. There was a hint of mockery in his voice that made Harry Stafford squirm, but it wasn't an unfriendly greeting.

In a dramatic gesture, Harry doffed his hat and went on one knee before Richard. He mourned the fact that the cobbles, clean as they were, would sully his new bright yellow hose, but alas, such losses were sometimes needed in the scheme of things. "Your Grace, I pray you will forgive my lateness in joining your Royal Progress. I was ill and taken to my bed, and then there was an urgent matter to attend to at Brecknock."

"I know…I received your letters," said Richard, a little shortly, and then, suddenly prodding Harry with the tip of his shoe, "Oh Harry, do get up. There is no need for this grovelling; I am not planning to punish you."

Buckingham sprang up, face reddening, all too aware of the choked laughter of Lovell and the rest. How dare they laugh at him…a Royal Duke! Of this company only Richard was his equal; he would take it from him, but not the others.

Richard had clearly seen his angry expression; his eyes grew cool, shaded by his lashes. He gestured for wine to be poured. "Rhenish," he said. "And it's good. Drink up, Harry, and stop sulking…it does not become you."

"Perhaps he learned that sour face from his Woodville wife!" joked Francis. The King said nothing. His companions laughed like a gaggle of foolish young squires.

Buckingham was furious at being the butt of Lovell's jest, but held his peace. He took the flagon and drained it then hastily started on another. Gradually, he was drawn into the group's conversation, which turned to more serious matters within a short time. He began to relax. It almost felt like old times again. Richard must have forgiven his rash and forward actions; surely he had realised by now his importance to his kingship. If not, he soon would. Surely there would be gratitude…and maybe the reward he wished for….They would be bound together by great deeds, far closer than brothers, far closer than Richard could be to that thin, dried-up slip he called a wife.

Sometime near midnight, Catesby, Ratcliffe and Lovell asked permission to depart and with Richard's leave headed for their beds or to the taprooms. Buckingham was left alone with Richard in the courtyard. The daylight was gone and the moon soared above the inn, casting a pallid sheen over the flagstones. The scent of the flowers hung heavy in the sultry summer air. Richard strode forward, his gown and hair and face silvered by the wavering light, the sapphires of his collar flashing blue fire on his breast. Buckingham almost choked on his wine at the sight. He looked almost surreal, an angel…a dark angel, perhaps even the angel of death, beautiful and terrible at the same time?

He halted before Harry, his face grave. "I am glad you are here," he said. "I thought mayhap…you were deserting my cause."

"I would never do that, your Grace!" Buckingham cried. "I can prove that to you! Cousin…Richard…I must speak with you, but not here, not in this public place, where many unfriendly ears might be listening."

Richard shook his head. "Tell me on the morrow, Harry. I have been riding long and my very bones ache. But know that I am truly glad to see you." He reached forward, tentatively, and gave Buckingham a quick, slightly awkward embrace. Buckingham's breath hissed through his teeth at the feel of his small, lean body against his, brief though contact was. A strand of Richard's hair brushed Harry's cheek—it felt like fine silk; he must have had it freshly washed that day. The scent of ambergris and thyme clung to his skin.

Buckingham reached up to clasp Richard's shoulder, as if to stop him from departing. Richard shook his head again and drew away. "Tomorrow."

Turning on his heel, the King left the courtyard through the arched doorway and did not glance back.

***

Richard sought out the rooms where the Queen was staying. Anne would not be sharing his bed that night or the next few nights because she had her monthly flux. Truth be told, he wasn't much bothered by such proprieties, he liked the feel of her slender limbs twined about his, but Anne was insistent she sleep alone. She had been upset when the bleeding started; she had half-convinced herself that she might be with child. He knew that when she sorrowed thus she believed that perhaps she was being punished with barrenness for their fleshly sins; for sometimes they gave way to lust and had relations on days forbidden by the church, and sometimes when he was saddle-sore and aching but in need of bodily release, he would not take the man's position of natural dominance but allowed Anne to straddle him, her long hair a veil cascading over them both, and ride his shaft until she shrieked with pleasure like some whore in the Southwark Stews and fell forward into his arms, spent.

He entered the chamber unannounced and all Anne's attending ladies, some with their heads uncovered, some in just their shifts as they readied to bed down, uttered coy little shrieks and tried to cover themselves. "Out!" the King said sternly, and they all scattered into the corridor, half-dressed or not.

Anne sat up in her bed, trying not to laugh. "Oh Richard, that was cruel!" she said. "They will be so embarrassed if anyone sees them!"

"I doubt that, Anne," said Richard. "Knowing that gaggle of hens, they'd probably be pleased."

He sat on the edge of the bed, gazing down. Again, he was struck by how frail Anne looked, with the light from the candle at the bedside glowing through her porcelain skin. He touched her face with his finger. "How are you, my lady?" he said quietly.

"Tired, that is all," she said, "and burdened with women's troubles. I had so hoped…" Her voice broke; she raised a hand to her mouth to stifle a sob.

"Don't think about it, Anne," he said, more sharply than he had intended. "It will happen if and when God wills it."

"But what if He doesn't will it?" She leaned forward and buried her face against his thigh.

"We have a son."

"But to pin all ones hopes on one small boy…and Edward, he is so small for his age. And he is sick so often…"

"I was small too…He is like me. And I was often ill as a child. Edward will be fine," said Richard stoutly. "Anne, don't take on so; it brings ill-luck when you speak such words."

He tried to change the subject. "At last Harry Stafford has shown up, Anne. Came riding into town this evening."

His announcement had the desired effect. Anne sat up, her look of dismay undisguised. "Oh has he? And you will accept him back after what he tried to do? After he did not come on progress when he should have? You don't surely believe his feigned illness, do you?"

"I told you, he is too important to my cause to drive away. Anne, his vice is something I have seen before, amongst soldiers when I have been at war. A grave sin it may be, but it does not make him unsound to have dealings with."

"It might if he …if he loves you beyond reason."

Richard flushed slightly. He remembered all too well Buckingham's pleading words after he had struck him for his presumption, for touching his royal person: *I love you, Richard.* "Anne, you women think too much about 'love,'" he murmured, his tone slightly mocking. "It is irrational and you let such irrationality rule you. He is a man, no matter his...proclivities, and I believe he will act as a man and lord of this realm and do his duty."

Anne said nothing. A small worried frown rose between her eyes. "You look tired." Richard brushed his lips against her cheek. "Sleep well...I do not want you to overtax yourself for fear that cough you suffer with will grow worse. I will come to you on the morrow and we will attend Mass."

***

Richard returned to his chamber in silence. Inside his young pages and squires, having finished preparing his wardrobe and turning back the rich coverlets on his bed, swarmed about him like an army of busy ants, unfastening his heavy garments, lifting off his gown, removing his doublet and hose and his under-linens. He felt unbearably hot; the night had grown sticky, and he gestured for them to wash him down to refresh him—this they did with scented water from a great silvered bowl they carefully placed on a mat on the floor.

After he had been cleansed to his satisfaction, the squires dried him with soft cloths, extinguished the candles around the room, and guided him to his bed. He dismissed them with a gesture as he slouched into the pillows and they scuttled away, eager to go about finding the kinds of excitement that young boys liked.

Was I ever that young? Richard thought wryly as he heard the last of their footfalls in the passage outside the door, and he turned over, coverlet drawn up to his waist, seeking sleep. Under the bolster his hand sought out the hilt of his dagger; he always kept it there, in every place he stayed, in the event of sudden assassination attempt in the night. It had an oddly comforting feel, the hard edge of cold steel softened by the feather-filled roll.

His eyes drifted shut and gradually he slept; a shaft of moonlight glancing through the open casement shone on his pale face, making him resemble a marble effigy, and his sleep look like the sleep of death. Somewhere above the rooftops of the town of Gloucester, an owl, a bird of ill-omen, hooted and then gave a great, eerie cry as it whirled down through the shadows to find its prey…

***

Richard awoke in the middle of the night. Half caught in the world of dream, he didn't quite remember where he was; he travelled so much, that was often the case: one inn or castle blurred into another. Glancing to the window, the moon had set; no light came through save that from a pallid blue star that twinkled in the firmament like a hard, watchful eye.

He shifted, trying to seek sleep again as it was still long before dawn and he needed rest his day would be full...but then he felt it. Fingers lightly tracing his buttock, his thigh, stroking gently. "Anne?" he murmured, his body responding instantly, forgetting in his sleep-befuddled state that she was not there. Breath warmed the back of his neck; he felt a mouth touch his flesh...then suddenly he realised that mouth was hard, not soft like Anne's, and the chin was rough, stubbled.

An oath tore from his mouth and he twisted to one side, reaching blindly in the dark for his dagger. It was not where he had left it!

As he tore the bolster from the bed, seeking his weapon, hands clamped down on his shoulders, throwing him face down on the bed. Although adrenaline surged through him like a tide, he could not move; his assailant was much heavier and broader than he was, his body lying heavy across his back.

"Don't look for the dagger...I took it from its hiding place. I knew where you kept it."

A voice drifted out of the dark and Richard recognised it at once. His blood ran cold. *Buckingham.* By God, did Harry mean to kill him, had he betrayed him, or was there more....

"Your life is forfeit!" he snarled. "How dare you touch me again, you sodomite! To touch the King without his permission is treason!"

Buckingham pressed him down onto the fine linen sheet, pinning his arms down at the wrists. "I've frightened you again, haven't I? Forgive me, forgive me...but I could not wait to talk to you tomorrow. I have so much to tell you, Richard...." He leaned forward; alcohol-soaked breath blasted into Richard's face, hot and spiced. Richard was suddenly reminded of his brother George, fickle, drunken, mad George; he wondered why he had not noticed the similarity to Harry Stafford before. "I have done a great deed for you, one that will ease your burdens. The crown will rest easier on your head from now onwards. I have taken this upon myself because of the love I feel for you. Just think of it, Dickon, together we can rule not only England...but we can take on the Scots, the French..."

"You're raving, man!" spat Richard. "Now I truly believe you have gone insane."

"Listen to me...I beg you..."

Richard managed to turn his head; he could see Buckingham's eyes shining in the gloom; they looked crazy, almost those of a man possessed.

"Let me up!" he spat. "And I will listen."

Buckingham loosened his hold slightly, enough so that Richard could partly turn and face him. "Speak!" Richard snarled.

"After that raid on the Tower when the rebels tried to free Edward's bastards, it became clear we had a serious problem. We almost lost those boys to our enemies. If certain factions got them as figureheads, we all could have our heads on the block within months."

"I am aware of that." Richard's mouth was a hard line.

"We spoke before...of what we might do. In the Tower."

"Yes." Richard's voice was sharp as steel. "We did. But talk was...talk. No decision was made."

"I made that decision for you," said Buckingham. "The sin, the evil....I have taken it upon myself, so that you a blameless before God and man." His eyes suddenly were awash with tears. "Does that not show you how deep my love is? Why do you reject me still?"

"Harry..." Richard's breath caught in his chest, suddenly his head reeled. What was Buckingham telling him? "Harry, what have you done? *What have you done?*"

Buckingham smiled, but it was a strange, twisted smile. "Dr Shaa said bastard slips would take no root. I have made sure of it, Richard. I have cut off the root before it has had chance to grow. Edward's byblows are both dead; I saw to it myself."

Richard stared at him, stunned to silence. Then he said in a low, shaking voice, "Look at me, *look at me*, Harry Stafford…"

Buckingham looked. A wave of cold was passing through him now, nullifying the affects of the alcohol he had imbibed. Richard's eyes. Gone the friendship. Gone the camaraderie. Any chance of any kind of love— gone too, gone forever. They had turned dark, almost black, the pupils huge in the dim room. The only expression in them was hate. Pure unadulterated hate. And revulsion, disgust, despair….He saw his own death in Richard's eyes and it terrified him.

The cold pang of fear fled almost immediately as anger surged within him. What an ungrateful bastard his cousin was! Buckingham had worked so hard to get him onto the throne, and this anger, this brutal rejection, was how he had repaid him? Maybe Morton was right; he, the Duke of Buckingham, would have made the better king…Well, he had made Richard, and so he could unmake him!

"I did the deed for *YOU*, don't you forget that, Richard," he spat between clenched teeth. "And if you think to have me killed for it…well, put that from your mind. I have messengers set along all the roads; if word comes to them that I am harmed they will ride all over the country and spread the news that you, the King, have ordered the deaths of your nephews, and that you murdered me when I objected to such a heinous crime. If you destroy me, I will bring about your downfall even in death! I can promise you that."

"You are a viper, Harry Stafford," Richard said, voice trembling with suppressed rage and emotion. "And to think you spoke to me of love."

"Hate is the other side of love, or so learned men say," Buckingham spat back, and though his tone was harsh and mocking, he found himself blinking back unbidden tears. He hoped Richard could not see them. "Now I will go, and return to my castle, and I expect to remain unmolested there. I would bid you remember what will happen if any action is taken against me, whether this be by arms or by stripping me of lands, titles, duties or money. Many factions are against you already; the news I could give them would unite them in open rebellion against you."

Richard turned ashen. "I could call out for my men and have you arrested, not killed. I could send you to the Tower for the rest of your miserable life—as you deserve!"

"But would you want others to witness our…meeting? Think of the scene here, my cousin…your men bursting in to find you naked in bed with another man! You would be a laughing stock, the catamite King! People would wonder if I had dishonoured you like some shrieking virgin…or if you fucking well enjoyed it. Your choice, Richard."

"Go then, you bastard," Richard hissed. "And do not ever seek to come into my presence again! I will expect you to carry out your duties as before, safe-guarding the west from our foes...but do not come to court, not ever again. If I ever hear that you have done anything more against me or mine, do not think I will hold my hand a second time!"

Harry sprang from the bed, flinging his discarded cloak around him. His hair was wild, his face a mask of rage and torment. "You are a fool, Richard!" he cried. "I did it for you. They were only Woodville brats!" He rushed from the chamber, slamming the door in fury; minutes later the sounds of a horse's frantically pounding hooves reverberated through the streets below.

Richard sat in the darkness, bowed over, holding his head in his hands. There was no point going after him. Harry did not make idle threats; were he apprehended he would make sure his vicious lies spread across England exactly as promised. News of the boy's deaths and other shameful tales would reach unfriendly ears; he would be ruined and despised and the land would go up in flames.

He had never really wanted the crown, not at first—had thought it was God's will for him to take the throne when it turned out Edward had pre-contracted marriage with Eleanor Butler. God's will that a legitimate Plantagenet heir sat on the throne, a grown man and seasoned soldier who could deal with England's enemies in a more fitting manner than an effete, cosseted young Woodville boy.

But now it felt like it had been Satan who had been whispering in his ear all along. And the devil wore the face of the Duke of Buckingham.

Author's note-

Henry Stafford, the 2nd Duke of Buckingham is an enigmatic character in the history of Richard III. A cousin of Richard and in line to the throne himself (some believe his claim was better than Henry Tudor's) he seemed to have been disliked or mistrusted by Edward IV, Richard's elder brother, as he was the only Duke without appointment. He was married to Elizabeth Woodville's sister but was rumoured to think the match beneath him because of his Royal blood.

He first emerged on the scene just after Edward had died and Richard was on his way to the south to assume his role as Lord Protector. Up to this point there was NO sign that Richard had any designs on the throne; he had made his men swear an oath to Edward V I and had brought only about 300 of them. Once he met with Buckingham, who promised him many men (but brought relatively few-he seemed something of an exaggerator), things started to change. Richard and Buckingham met up with Anthony Woodville, Lord Rivers, in Northampton, and were probably rather startled that he did not have the young Prince Edward with him as promised…the boy was in Stony Stratford with an armed force, some miles further south. Nonetheless, despite this change of plans, they dined with Woodville, amiably enough it seems. However, the next morning Rivers and others were arrested. Later, these men were executed for treason.

Over the coming weeks Buckingham continued to support Richard and supported his claim for the throne, and was rewarded richly for it in titles and positions.

And then things get rather strange. First Buckingham reportedly does not accompany the King on his progress but stays on for several days in London. Later, at the beginning of August he meets Richard in Gloucester, where, it is thought, they have some kind of argument or disagreement. They part, never to speak again, though Richard continues to pay money to Buckingham's account till September and even asks him to see about rumours of risings and unrest in the west.

In October Stafford mounts a full rebellion, prompted most likely by Bishop John Morton, an enemy of Richard's who was imprisoned at Buckingham's castle. It is first raised in the name of Edward V and then switched to Henry Tudor. This is quite interesting as the change in figureheads implies that it is positively known Edward V is dead, but Richard was not even in London at this time and this change of allegiance seems to imply inside knowledge.

Buckingham's rebellion soon floundered, in part due to terrific storms and the flooded Severn. He was captured, turned in by one of his own, and beheaded for treason in the market place in Salisbury. A tomb that may have been his stands in Britford church.

Some think Buckingham may have been aiming for the throne himself. If it had been relatively easy to put Richard there, why not himself? It seems unlikely he would have truly followed Tudor; he may well have planned to use his men, and then turn on him as well. And could Buckingham have killed the Princes (if, indeed, they were killed at all.) Yes. He had motive and he had opportunity

In the 1980's a document was in fact discovered that stated the Princes in the Tower were killed 'by the vice of the Duke of Buckingham.' Whether this means advice or device we do not know. Several other documents, including ones found on the continent, also mention him as the potential murderer, though they may have copied an original. Legend has it that the Duke either had them taken from the Tower and drowned, or locked them away and let them starve. I have set their disappearance in late July but there may be some reference to them still being alive in late August/early September; however it may have taken some time for the actual knowledge that they were no long in the Tower to seep to the outside world.

I do not believe the bones found in the 1600's at the Tower are the Princes but are more likely to be from the Roman and Iron Age settlements once on Tower hill. If the Princes died, I suspect their bodies are elsewhere.

****

This story is a work of fiction and it is also meant to be a wee bit erotic. The idea that Buckingham might have been gay is not mine; it has been around for more than a few years and alluded to, very gently, in a few other fiction pieces. A scholarly paper was written some years ago that did suggest that perhaps Richard and Buckingham were involved in a swift, intense relationship, and that is why Buckingham's star rose so very suddenly...and fell so far. However, at 31, it hardly seems likely that Richard is going to unexpectedly discover he prefers men; he seems to have been faithful to Anne, his wife, as far as we know, but he did father several illegitimate children in his youth—up to 7 according to some authors, though only two are positively documented.

I hope no one is offended by the subject of my story or think that I have in any way further maligned King Richard, whose reputation suffered so horribly after his death. Even his looks were trashed by the subsequent Tudor dynasty; despite suffering scoliosis (which is NOT a 'hunchback!'); he in reality appears to have been a very good-looking man. I admire the positive aspects of his brief reign very much and hope that he soon shall have the fitting and respectful burial that was denied him after Bosworth, as well as renewed study into his life and character.

M.M.

Printed in Great Britain
by Amazon